Night Owls

by Sharon Phillips Denslow
illustrated by Jill Kastner

Bradbury Press   New York

To Kim and Mary Ellen,
 who were night owls with me,
Tony, Erin, and Kate,
 who are the real night owls,
and to Virginia,
 who had to have the deer!
                    —S.P.D.

For Dilys and all the
Aunt Kays of the world.
Thanks.
                    —J.K.

When all the other houses on her road are dark,
Charlene's house is not.
"There's a little bit of magic in a cake baked at night," she says.

If the neighbors hear the CRUNCH, CRUNCH, CRUNCH
of someone walking down the road, they know it is
Charlene walking her dog, Emmett, at midnight.

Charlene is a night owl. She has always been
afraid she will miss something wonderful
if she goes to bed too early.

Charlene's favorite nights are
in midsummer when her nephew
William comes to visit.

"We're two of a kind," she tells him.

This year, they decide to celebrate their reunion
with a night picnic.
"Let's have a bonfire!" William suggests.
"And corn on the cob and raspberries!"
"We just might find a roasting ear or two," Charlene says.

"Come on, Emmett!"

Charlene and William take a basket to the garden
to check the tiny ears of corn.
"Here's one ready," Charlene calls.
"Here's another one," William says.
They find six ears big enough to eat and
two sets of deer tracks across the
corner of the garden.

"When did those tracks get there?" William wants to know.
"Oh, late some night when Emmett wasn't looking,"
Charlene says.

"Charlene! He's eating all the raspberries!"

Emmett noses the soft, round berries off the bushes
more quickly than Charlene and William can pick them.
"Move over, Emmett!" Charlene says. "We want some, too!"

At dusk, they sit on the back steps eating corn
and raspberries and drinking lemonade.
William's bonfire glows.
As it gets darker, Charlene keeps a tight hold on Emmett
so he won't chase the skunks and rabbits who might want
to explore the garden.

The yard slowly fills with lightning bugs.
Charlene and William count twenty-three
different cricket and frog voices singing their
night songs.

"William," Charlene says suddenly. "Let's climb that tree!"
"Now? In the dark?" William asks.
"Why not?" Charlene says. She boosts William up
onto a low branch. "Hold on tight."

Below them, in the yard, the lightning bugs shine,
and above them, between dark clusters of summer leaves,
the stars grow thicker and thicker.

"I've got bubbles!" remembers William.
Together Charlene and William blow soap bubbles,
decorating the night.

"You know what we are, William?" Charlene asks. "Night owls!"
And William laughs and hoots across the dark,
adding his voice to the other night songs.

When all the other houses on her road are dark,
Charlene's house is not.
Chances are, she is writing a letter to William.
She doesn't want him to miss something wonderful.

"Three deer came marching up the driveway last night.
Emmett was so surprised, he didn't even bark!"

"*Do you think it snows more at night than it does during the day?*"

*"Oh, William, I can hear the first spring peeper
at the edge of the berry thicket
where we picked raspberries!"*

"It is like summer tonight.
Soon the lightning bugs will be here. And so will you.
And there will be two night owls together again."

Bradbury Press, An Affiliate of Macmillan, Inc.
866 Third Avenue, New York, NY 10022, Collier Macmillan Canada, Inc.

The text of this book is set in New Aster Semi Bold. The illustrations are rendered in pastels.
Typography by Julie Quan

Printed and bound by South China Printing Company, Hong Kong
First American Edition 10 9 8 7 6 5 4 3 2 1

Library of Congress Cataloging-in-Publication Data
Denslow, Sharon Phillips.
Night owls/by Sharon Phillips Denslow; illustrated by Jill Kastner.—1st ed.
p.   cm.
Summary: William and his aunt, both night owls, stay up late and experience
the wonder of a midsummer night.
ISBN 0-02-728681-9
[1. Night—Fiction. 2. Aunts—Fiction.] I. Kastner, Jill, ill.   II. Title.
PZ7.D433Ni   1990   [E]—dc20   89-33937 CIP AC